Jacob's Trouble

PRAISE FOR *STORYSHARES*

"One of the brightest innovators and game-changers in the education industry."
– Forbes

"Your success in applying research-validated practices to promote literacy serves as a valuable model for other organizations seeking to create evidence-based literacy programs."

- Library of Congress

"We need powerful social and educational innovation, and Storyshares is breaking new ground. The organization addresses critical problems facing our students and teachers. I am excited about the strategies it brings to the collective work of making sure every student has an equal chance in life."
– Teach For America

"Around the world, this is one of the up-and-coming trailblazers changing the landscape of literacy and education."
- International Literacy Association

"It's the perfect idea. There's really nothing like this. I mean wow, this will be a wonderful experience for young people."   - Andrea Davis Pinkney, Executive Director, Scholastic

"Reading for meaning opens opportunities for a lifetime of learning. Providing emerging readers with engaging texts that are designed to offer both challenges and support for each individual will improve their lives for years to come. Storyshares is a wonderful start."
- David Rose, Co-founder of CAST & UDL

Jacob's Trouble

Kelly Winters

STORYSHARES

Story Share, Inc.
New York. Boston. Philadelphia

Storyshares
Story Share, Inc.
24 N. Bryn Mawr Avenue #340
Bryn Mawr, PA 19010-3304
www.storyshares.org

Inspiring reading with a new kind of book.

Interest Level: High School
Grade Level Equivalent: 2.4

9781973448310

Book design by Storyshares

Printed in the United States of America

Storyshares Presents

1

Lupe Morales liked me. It was a miracle.

Lupe was a straight-A student, the smartest kid in school. She could read in Spanish or English. She could write in both languages. She had even won awards for her stories. And for her photos. She wanted to be a news reporter, so she took a camera and a notebook everywhere.

I was not a straight-A student. Not even straight-B! I was lucky if I was straight-C. When I tried to read, the words kept moving around. The letters were always jumping. I couldn't remember things I read. If someone read to me, then it was better. But in school, they expected you to read everything yourself. Not be read to like a little kid. So I had problems.

But Lupe didn't care. She actually liked me!

I once asked her why she liked me. She said, "You're a good person, Jacob. You're solid. You're honest. And I do think you're smart. Not school smart, but smart at other things."

I didn't think so, but I was sure glad she did. I called her Loop for short, because when she wasn't writing or taking pictures, she was knitting. Making loops with yarn. Loop after loop after loop. Add them all up, and they turned into sweaters. She was so good that she could knit in the dark, without even looking at her hands.

"Why do you knit all the time?" I once asked her.

"I hate doing nothing," she said. "Knitting keeps me busy. And I like what I make."

"I like what you make, too," I said. She was wearing a sweater she made. It looked great on her!

Her parents owned a store on South Broad Street, the main street in our town. They sold Mexican groceries. I loved the delicious smells in that store. Her mother made enchiladas, tacos, and tamales. She sold them to workers who were far from home, far away from their families back in Mexico. Every day at lunchtime there was a line down the block.

When I started going out with Lupe, my mother told me, "I know this is your first real girlfriend. She's a nice, smart girl. And I don't want to hear about any trouble with her. You better behave yourself. If you know what I mean."

"I know what you mean," I said.

My mother didn't have to worry. Lupe's brother Geraldo had muscles on top of muscles. He told me, "If you ever make my sister cry, your face will never look the same. You will have to eat all your food without any teeth. If you know what I mean."

"I know what you mean," I said. And I treated her like the queen she was.

2

Before Lupe's parents opened their store, my mom, my dad, and her parents worked together at The Mill. Everyone in town called it The Mill. Most people in town either worked there, or had someone in their family who worked there.

A long time ago, it was a knitting mill. They made underwear and t-shirts. Did you know that underwear is knitted? It is. If you look at it close up, you can see the little tiny loops. Like Lupe's sweaters, but much smaller.

But the knitting mill closed and it turned into a plastic factory. They made the plastic boxes that car batteries go in. It was a smaller factory, so some of the workers lost their jobs.

My mom was one of them. She kept looking for another job. She got one working at the donut shop.

Lupe's parents lost their jobs, too. That was when they opened their store.

My dad kept working at the plastic factory. He fixed all the machines there, so they couldn't run the place without him.

But after a few months, he started getting more and more tired. "You're working too much," my mom told him.

"I just need to get a good night's sleep," he said.

He got a good night's sleep, and he was still tired. Tired, and quiet, like there were things he couldn't say. He was thinner, too. No matter how much he ate, he got skinnier and skinnier.

***

Finally, he went to the doctor. They kept him in the hospital. They said they were going to do some tests.

The next day was Saturday. My mom was quiet. I could tell she had something on her mind.

"Today we're going to the hospital to see your dad," was all she said.

"OK," I said.

I didn't like going to the hospital. It made me nervous. I hated that hospital smell. That bandaid-smelling, medicine-smelling, people-are-sick-in-here smell.

I was worried about my dad. What was wrong with him?

3

When we got to the hospital, my dad was in a room by himself, with a plastic bag of medicine attached to a pole next to him. The clear liquid dripped slowly through a tube, from the bag into his arm.

I sat on the edge of a green chair. My dad was sleeping. I patted his skinny arm. "Hi, Dad."

He didn't wake up. He just slept.

A doctor came in. She was holding a folder full of papers. "Mrs. Gardner?"

My mom stood up.

"And, uh..." She looked at a folder of papers she was carrying. "Jacob?"

"Yeah," I said. I stood up, too.

"No, no, you can sit down. Please. Thank you for bringing your son in today, Mrs. Gardner. I'm glad we have this chance to talk."

We sat down. She started talking. All kinds of medical stuff. Names of medicines, tests, different kinds of x-rays to look inside my dad's body. The one word that made it into my head was this one:

CANCER.

I stopped thinking when I heard it. Stopped listening. It was like everything inside me just froze.

Cancer?

"Is he going to die?" I interrupted.

The doctor looked at me. Right into my eyes. "We don't know," she said. "He is very ill. But we'll do everything we can to help him."

My mother started crying.

I just stayed frozen.

The doctor kept talking. She said that once they figured out the right treatment for my dad, he could probably come home from the hospital. Nurses could come visit him at the house. For a while, though, he would stay in the hospital.

He had already been in a lot of pain at home and now he was finally getting relief from it. That was what the bag of medicine on the pole was. Pain relief.

Now I knew why he had been so quiet. He had been in pain, but he didn't want us to know.

"Can't you, like, operate on him and take it out?" I asked.

"No. Unfortunately, the cancer has spread too much. We can't take it out without taking out too many of the organs he needs."

I actually don't remember much after that. Don't remember driving home, or talking to my mom, or going to bed.

In the middle of the night, I woke up.

What am I feeling? I asked myself.

What I felt was scared. Really scared, because he was sick. Because he might die.

But I didn't want to be scared. It was scary to be scared. So instead, I got mad. Really mad. Mad that my dad was sick. Mad that he might die.

I got up in the dark and got dressed. Put on my socks and shoes. Went into the hall.

Opened the door, and went outside.

All was quiet. Everyone was sleeping but me.

I had never been outside by myself in the middle of the night before. Normally, I would have been kind of worried to be out on the street alone in the dark, but cancer was scarier.

And it made me so mad that I wasn't scared of the dark anymore.

I went down the street. Walked a few blocks. I found myself in an alley behind an old, run-down building that no one used anymore.

Someone had broken one of its windows.

I wondered how it would feel to smash a window like that. Before I knew it, I had a rock in my hand. That was one thing I was good at. I could throw and hit anything I wanted to, pretty much every time. I had been good at that since I was little.

I threw the rock. It hit the window just right.

Smash! The sound echoed down the street.

Man, did that feel good. It was like I was breaking my dad's cancer. Breaking my fear. I wished I could do another one. But I didn't want to get caught. So I ran.

Back home, back inside, pajamas on, pretending to be asleep. I lay there with my eyes closed tight, trying hard to sleep. Trying to close my eyes so tight that no tears could get out.

I thought about my dad for the longest time. Then, finally, I fell asleep for real.

4

On Monday, my English teacher, Mr. Kloot, stood with his arms folded. "Jacob. In the book To Kill a Mockingbird, do all the characters have an equal chance to have life, liberty, and the pursuit of happiness?"

"Uh, they... I don't know."

"Did you read the book, Jacob?"

"Uh, no."

"Jacob," he said. "See me after class."

He asked me why I hadn't done my homework.

I didn't want to tell him about my dad. I was not a crying kind of guy, but if I told him about my dad, I might cry. So I just folded my arms and looked down and didn't say anything when he asked.

"Since you seem to like being quiet, I'll give you some reasons to be quiet. Three of them. I expect three book reports by next Friday. All that reading should give you enough quiet time."

Oh, just shoot me now, I wanted to say. Read three books by next week! He might as well ask me to fly to the moon.

"Long books?" I asked. "How many pages?"

"Here's a list of books. Pick three of these." He slapped a piece of paper into my hand.

It was a long list. Full of long, long books. Just great.

* * *

That afternoon, when we went to the hospital, my dad was awake. The sun was shining through his window. It reflected off the silvery medicine pole and lit up all the flowers that people from The Mill had sent him.

Even though he was so sick, he tried to make me laugh.

"Jacob, remember the time we went fishing and I caught your line? I kept trying to reel you in. I thought I had the biggest fish in the world."

"Jacob, remember the time we got up at midnight to watch the shooting stars? And we thought we saw a UFO?"

"Jacob, remember when you were little and you asked me what your belly button was? And I told you it was a screw that holds your butt onto your body?"

I laughed at that one, but it hurt at the same time. Hurt because maybe this time next year, he wouldn't be around to make these jokes with me.

When I was little, he used to crawl around on his hands and knees and let me ride him like a horse. I would grab his hair and kick his sides and he would just laugh.

He used to throw me in the air. I remember the world spinning and then he'd catch me. He always had time for me. He was the strongest, safest, best dad in the world.

I looked at him now, in his hospital bed with the light blue sheets and the plastic bags of medicine dripping into his skinny arm.

I tried to smile.

5

When my dad wasn't working at The Mill, he was in his workshop behind our house, making things. He made furniture. Bookcases, tables, chairs. Our house was full of beautiful things that he made. He sold them, too. Lots of people in town had furniture he had built.

After school the next day, while my mom was working at the donut shop, I went into his workshop and sat on his stool.

He had just started making a dresser for my mom. He had a stack of beautiful pieces of wood all ready for it. On top of them was a sheet of paper with drawings and numbers. All the measurements he would need to make the dresser and the drawers.

On the wall, he had racks of tools. Each tool had a black outline traced around it with a marker. When you took a tool off the wall, the empty outline reminded you to put the tool back when you were done. It was very orderly.

Looking at the wall, with the black outlines all filled in with the right tools, always made me feel good. Safe. Nice and orderly.

Him being sick made me feel unsafe. Him being in the hospital was like having the hammer missing from the rack.

An empty outline on the wall.

6

That night, I didn't read any of the books for my English assignment. I didn't do my math homework, and I didn't do my history homework, either. I sat in my room, feeling mad, watching the clock.

When my mom was asleep, I snuck out again.

I went back to the empty old building. I saw the two broken windows: one I had done, and one from someone before me. I picked up a rock and threw it.

Smash! Three broken windows in a row. Tic-tac-toe. I win.

Get lost, cancer.

Someone stepped out from around the side of the building. The streetlight shone on the top of his big head and wide shoulders.

It was Nathan Sprague. I knew him from school. He was a tough kid. A bully. He had never bothered me before, but I didn't like him.

"The cops would love to hear about how all those windows got broken," he said.

I just stared at him. Man, was I stupid to get caught doing this. Stupid, stupid!

"You could spend the rest of your life in jail."

Was that true? I had no idea.

He would know. He had already been to juvenile jail. Twice.

"But I know a way you can keep it a secret."

"How?"

"Come with me."

He took me around the side of the building. We walked a few blocks to an alley behind some stores. Two other kids were there, smoking behind a garbage bin. Steve Schlager and AJ Pelland. Two more bullies. I didn't like them, either.

I had made it all the way through school without them bothering me. That was a miracle. Now, my miracle was over.

They gave me dirty looks as Nathan pushed me over to them.

"What's this loser doing here?" Pelland asked.

He threw down his cigarette butt. He had a crowbar in one hand. For a second, I thought he was going to hit me with it.

"This loser can throw," Nathan told them.

He pushed my shoulder and turned me around.

"Ok, loser. See the security camera above the back door of that store? Throw this brick and smash it. Otherwise, we'll break your arm. It's so simple, even someone as stupid as you can understand it. Got it?"

He handed me a brick. Then the three of them stood, arms folded, watching me.

I looked at the camera, figuring how far it was and how hard to throw. If I didn't do it, they would break my arm. And tell the cops about the windows, and send me to jail.

I threw the brick. The camera smashed. Pieces of it fell to the ground. I stayed hunched down behind the garbage bin.

They ran toward the door of the store. I heard them jamming the crowbar into the lock and breaking it open. Then they ran into the store.

I stayed behind the garbage bin, afraid to move.

They came out, throwing a bunch of candy bars and cigarettes at me as they ran past. "Move, stupid!" one of them said.

I picked up the stuff they threw at me and ran. My stomach hurt. I passed another garbage bin and threw all of the stuff into it. I hated smoking. And stolen candy just didn't sound that delicious.

At home, my mother was still sleeping. The house was all dark.

I was so nervous that I was shaking. My stomach was killing me. I went into the bathroom and threw up. Then I got into bed. It took a long time before my heart stopped pounding. Every time a car drove by, I thought it was the police coming to get me.

When the sun came up, I fell asleep. But an hour later, my alarm went off. Time to go to school.

7

At school, Nathan came up behind me in the hall and twisted my arm up behind my back. It hurt. A lot.

"Remember what I told you," Nathan said. "Keep your mouth shut. Oh, and meet us at the same place at midnight tonight."

Tonight? Were they going to make me do this stuff every night?

"Be there, or you're dead," he said.

* * *

At midnight, I was there.

That night, we didn't steal anything. We just smashed things. I smashed six windows.

The night after that, I broke two more windows and spray-painted a curse word on the brick wall behind the car wash.

The three bullies gave me high fives.

"I thought you were such a loser," Steve Pelland told me. "But now I'm thinking you might be cool."

Breaking things with Nathan and his buddies was scary. But in a strange way, it was also exciting. That weekend, they stopped calling me "Loser" and started calling me "Catapult" because of my throwing. Finally, I was good at something.

I started feeling better about what we were doing because no one was catching us. It seemed like no one was even trying.

It kind of made me feel smart, doing this stuff and not getting caught. Like we were smarter than adults. Smarter than cops. It was a rush.

It felt like winning a game. Yeah! It was almost like we should have cheerleaders jumping up and down and waving pom poms every time we got away with something. Like everyone else in the world was stupid, because they were home sleeping while we were out breaking things. Stupid people. Too stupid to guard their stuff against us.

I was just mad, and throwing bricks and hitting things so perfectly made me feel better. For a second. But one second of feeling better was better than not feeling better at all.

But other times, racing down dark streets, hearing dogs bark in people's houses as we ran by, I would know: This isn't going to make my dad any better.

And I would try not to think about it, as I picked up another rock.

* * *

On Monday, in school, Lupe came up to me in the hall.

"What are you hanging around with those guys for?" she asked.

"What guys?"

"That Nathan and his friends. They're bad news."

I agreed with her, but I couldn't tell her that. "Oh, they're OK."

"No, they're not. They came into our store last week and stole stuff. One of them kept my dad busy, and the other ones put things under their jackets and walked out."

"Did you call the cops?"

"No, because we couldn't prove they did it. We don't have a security camera. But now my dad wants to get one. Also, I think they're racist. I've heard them say things about Mexicans that I don't like. I don't have time for people like that. No way. If you keep hanging around with them, I don't think I can hang around with you."

"But Loop, I…"

"Nope. I don't spend my time with dirtbags." And she was gone.

8

Every afternoon, after school, I went to see my dad. Sometimes I went with my mom, but if she was working, I rode my bike and went by myself.

Sometimes my dad was awake. Sometimes he was asleep. I didn't care. I just wanted to be with him. I hated leaving the hospital at nine o'clock when they made all the visitors go home.

I just missed him. And it hurt. A lot.

* * *

In the middle of the school week, after running around with the guys, I came home at 2:30 in the morning.

My mother was up. She was sitting in the kitchen, waiting for me. Uh-oh.

"Jacob, I was worried. Where were you?"

I didn't answer.

"Were you at Lupe's?"

"No," I said. "She broke up with me."

"She did? Why?"

This was good. At least she was distracted from asking where I had been.

"She doesn't like some guys I was hanging out with. She thinks they're dirtbags."

"Are they?" She asked.

I didn't answer at first. Then I said, "Yeah, they are. They're bad news."

"Is that who you were with?"

"Yeah."

"Are you doing drugs?"

"No, mom, I swear I'm not."

"What are you doing with them, then?"

I didn't answer.

She said, "Jacob, if you're hanging out with troublemakers, maybe you should go talk to Uncle Cliff. He'll tell you what happens to boys like that."

I already knew.

My mother's brother, my Uncle Cliff, was a prison guard in Auburn, a couple of towns away. He loved to tell me stories about the guys in jail. He had millions of these stories because he had worked there all his life.

Most of the stories were sad. Some of them were scary. Some of them were funny, but only if you weren't in them. Or in the prison. No way did I ever want to go there.

***

By Thursday, school was a blur. I was so tired. Mr. Kloot asked me where my book reports were.

I hadn't even gotten the books from the library yet.

"Uh, Mr. Kloot, I think I need a little more time."

He gave me a mean look. "OK, Jacob, I'm giving you one more chance. You can have the weekend to work on them. Have them on my desk by Monday."

I couldn't wait to get out of there.

9

After school that day, my mom was working at the donut shop, so I rode my bike to the hospital to see my dad.

On the little table next to him was a picture of him, my mom, and me at Franklin Lake. He loved that picture. My mom must have brought it in to cheer him up.

Last summer, my dad took me to Franklin Lake. It's a big, huge lake with wide beaches. You can go parasailing there. You put on a parachute and hook up a long rope to a fast boat. When the boat takes off, you lift up in the air like a kite.

It's amazing, but also very expensive. I had always wanted to do it. We could never afford it. My dad saw me watching the people flying.

"Jacob. Want to fly?"

"Well, yeah, but isn't it too expensive?"

"No. If you want to do it, I'll pay."

"I don't know, Dad. It's a lot of money."

Before I knew it, he was talking to the guy in the boat. Then I was standing in water up to my ankles, with a harness strapped around my body and a long rope going to the boat. My heart was pumping. The guys in the boat gave me a thumbs-up sign: Ready?

I gave them a thumbs-up back. I looked at my dad. He waved and gave me a thumbs-up.

The guys in the boat hit the gas and just like that, I was flying. It was amazing! I lifted up in the air and couldn't stop laughing. It was the most incredible thing I had ever felt.

Down on the beach, everyone looked small. I could see the sunlight rippling on the water, people swimming... they looked like colored sprinkles. Tiny toy people on the beach, tiny toy cars driving on the road. Blue sky and puffy clouds above me, blue water below. Wow.

On the beach, my dad stood with his head tilted way back, watching me. Watching me, and waving.

I waved back and yelled, "Dad! This is awesome!"

When my flight was over, the boat slowed and stopped. I came floating gently down. I landed standing up in shallow water, almost exactly where I had started.

My dad was waiting for me. He gave me a huge hug and pounded my back.

"Dad! That was incredible! Wow!" I was still laughing.

On the way home, I was tired but happy. I looked over at my dad as he drove. I couldn't believe he had paid for me to do that.

"Thanks, Dad," I said.

He reached over and gave me a fake-punch on the shoulder. A friendly punch. He had a huge smile on his face. Almost as if he was the one who had flown.

* * *

Now, he showed me the picture. "Remember this, Jacob?"

"Yeah. It was awesome. I can't believe you did that, Dad. It must have cost your whole paycheck."

"Jacob," he said. "Last summer was when I started feeling sick. I kind of knew something big was wrong with me. I didn't tell anyone, but I was afraid I had cancer because I was so tired and I was losing so much weight. I decided that if I was going to die, I wanted to see you fly before I went."

I just stared at him. "Dad, you're not gonna die..."

"Jacob, I have to be honest with you. I might. So I have to tell you this. You're my son. I've loved you since before you were born. You're the greatest thing that ever happened to me."

I looked at the floor. If he knew what I was doing at night, he wouldn't say that.

He said, "I wanted to see you fly. Jacob, that was one of the happiest days of my life. I loved seeing you so happy up there."

He paused, and looked out the window at the sky. "I'm so glad I got to see that, Jacob. See my son fly, like an eagle, before I die."

10

When I got home from the hospital, my mom wasn't home yet. There was a cooler sitting on our front steps. A note was taped to the top of it. It was from Lupe's mom.

Dear Mrs. Gardner, Lupe told me Mr. Gardner was sick. I thought you might not have time to cook. I hope you enjoy this supper.

I picked up the cooler and brought it into the kitchen. It was full of hot, delicious-smelling Mexican food. A big tray of enchiladas. A container of fresh salsa. Homemade tortillas. Tacos. And a bunch of different Mexican sodas.

The labels were all in Spanish:

Jarritos

Topo Sabores

Tamarindo

When my mom came home from work, I showed her the cooler. She gave a big sigh of relief about not having to cook, because she was really tired.

"That whole family is so nice," my mom said, as we ate. "You picked the right girl, Jacob. I hope you can work it out with her."

I hoped so, too.

My mom and I sat at our kitchen table and ate and ate. The food was delicious. It felt so good to eat. It felt like someone cared about us.

We sampled all the sodas. We pretended we were on one of those cooking shows, where they say ridiculous things about wine.

"A rich, fruity aroma," I said. I swirled the soda around in my glass and sniffed it, like the people on TV.

"A nice bouquet. A fine vintage," my mom said.

We both started laughing. It was like old times, before my dad got sick.

But then, as I drank my soda, I saw my dad's empty chair at the kitchen table. I wished he could be here to eat this supper with us. I looked at my mom, and I could tell she was thinking the same thing.

* * *

I called Lupe's house. She picked up the phone.

"Hi, Loop," I said.

"Don't call me Loop," she said. "I'm not talking to you."

"I wanted to thank you for the cooler."

She said, "That was for your mom. Not you. My mom and I wanted to help your mom out. I'm mad at you."

"But Lupe..."

"I don't want to hear it. I don't talk to dirtbags." Then she hung up.

* * *

The next morning at school, Nathan grabbed my arm and pulled me into a corner in the hall. AJ and Steve were there.

Nathan said, "We're gonna smash the Mexican place."

I said, "What Mexican place?"

"The store, idiot. Your little girlfriend's place. The only Mexican place. They probably have a lot of cash in there."

My stomach hurt. I felt like I was going to throw up. Lupe's parents' store!

"Tonight. Be in the alley behind South Broad Street at midnight."

I was quiet.

Nathan punched me in the shoulder. "You better not get any ideas about bailing out on us," he said. "Because if you do, you're dead."

11

English was my last class of the day. It was the only class that Lupe was in with me. I kept trying to get her to look at me.

She wouldn't. She kept her head turned away. She acted like her book was the most interesting thing in the world. For her, it probably was. She sure did love to read.

Finally, I decided to write her a note.

Mr. Kloot was writing on the board in front of the class.

While he was turned around, I tore a page out of my notebook and wrote:

Lupe, I know you can't stand me anymore, but this is important. Something bad is going on. Nathan Sprague and his buddies are going to break into your store. We have to stop it. Please help me. Be at your store at midnight tonight. Bring your camera. Bring your brother! If you see anything, take as many pictures as you can.

I folded up the note and passed it to my buddy Craig Seaborne, who sat next to me.

"Love note for me?" he said.

I rolled my eyes and jerked my head toward Lupe, who sat on the other side of him. But as he was leaning over to give it to her, Mr. Kloot turned around.

"Give me the note, Craig."

Craig looked at me and shrugged. He handed the note to Mr. Kloot.

Mr. Kloot crumpled it up without reading it and threw it in the wastebasket next to his desk. I wanted to slam my head against my desk.

I kept trying to get Lupe to look at me, but she wouldn't. And when class was over, she went and stood next to Mr. Kloot's desk with her friend Rosa.

I couldn't talk to her in front of him. I didn't want him to notice me. He would ask me about those book reports. I hadn't even gotten the books yet.

I went out into the hall to wait for Lupe.

Nathan was out there. As soon as I came through the classroom door, he grabbed my arm and twisted it behind my back. It hurt so much I thought he was going to break it.

"Walk this way," he said. He pushed me down the hallway to a little corner, then slammed me up against the cinderblock wall. "Be there tonight," he said. "Or I'll be waiting for you. And after I get through with you, there will be nothing left."

By the time I got back to Mr. Kloot's room, Lupe was gone.

12

When I got home, I called the store. Geraldo answered.

"Is Lupe there?" I asked.

"Not for you, she isn't," he said.

"OK, Geraldo, listen, I have to tell you..."

"Goodbye," he said, "We don't talk to racists." Then he hung up.

I called back, but as soon as he heard my voice, he hung up again. I walked over there.

Geraldo was standing behind the counter. He was talking to a cop. A big, burly cop. The cop's name was Officer Dassler. Lupe had told me about him. His mother was Mexican. He missed her home cooking, so he came into the store every afternoon to buy his dinner from Mrs. Morales.

I could tell Officer Dassler about the break-in, but when he found out about all the other things I had done, he would arrest me. I turned around and ran home. I would have to think of something else.

By the time midnight came, I hadn't thought of anything else. If I didn't show up, Nathan would come and kill me. So I showed up.

I met the bullies in the alley behind Lupe's parents' store. We stayed behind a pile of old fruit and vegetable boxes, and peeked out at the store.

A little light shone above the door. It reflected off some cases of glass bottles that were stacked next to the door, waiting to be recycled. Mexican soda bottles, like the ones Lupe's mother had sent over to us.

Inside the store, it was dark. In the little office room upstairs, all the shades were down. No lights were on.

"Listen, uh, I don't think this is such a good idea," I said.

"Why not?"

"What if we get caught?"

"We're not gonna get caught. They don't even have a security camera."

"Yeah, but what if we leave fingerprints or something."

"We won't. You might, because we're gonna make you open the door." He laughed. He shoved the crowbar into my hand. "OK," he said. "Walk over there and jam the crowbar into the crack between the door and the wall. Then push to the left as hard as you can. See if you can break the lock."

I looked at him in the dim light. His eyes were shining. He was so happy that I was a dirtbag now, too. It wasn't enough for him that I was breaking things. Now he wanted me to steal, too. From my girlfriend's family.

I thought of my dad, telling me he wanted me to fly like an eagle. If he knew I was doing this, he would really be disappointed and angry with me. My mom would kill me.

And I would hate myself. I never wanted to do any of this stuff. I had just let myself get sucked into it. It hadn't made my dad any better. And now it wasn't making me feel better, either.

Also, if I let them keep making me do these things, I really would be a dirtbag. It would never end. I would spend my whole life doing stupid things just because other stupid people told me to.

Getting arrested didn't seem so bad, now. It was better than being dead. If I got arrested, that was just the price I had to pay. I could stop doing these things. Maybe the cops would help me if I told them I wanted to stop hanging out with Nathan and his gang.

I looked right at him. I said, "I'm not doing it, Nathan. And I don't care if you beat me up. I don't care if you tell the cops about all those windows I broke."

13

His eyes opened wide, like he couldn't believe I just said that to him.

I took off my shirt.

"What are you undressing for?" he asked. "You wanna fight?"

I wrapped my shirt around the handle of the crowbar, so I wouldn't leave any fingerprints.

Then I raised the crowbar and threw it like a spear, right at the case of empty glass bottles. My shirt fell off in midair, but the crowbar kept sailing straight at the bottles.

SMASH! I hit them perfectly. The bottles broke into a zillion pieces. The sound was huge. Surely someone would hear it and call the cops!

Nathan punched me in the face. "Idiot! What are you doing?" He punched me again, so hard I fell down, then jumped on me and kept punching me, cursing and smashing his big fist into my face.

I rolled sideways to get away from him. He jumped on me again, pounding and pounding. I tried to kick him off. Steve and AJ grabbed him and pulled him off me.

"Forget this loser, you're wasting time, let's get some stuff before anyone comes," AJ said. He ran to the door and picked up the crowbar.

I sat up, feeling blood spurt out my nose, tasting it in my mouth. I felt dizzy.

They were pushing the crowbar, trying to break the door open. Finally, it broke. It opened wide.

FLASH! A bright light, like lightning, filled up the doorway. Then again: FLASH! FLASH!

In the bright flash, I saw Lupe, standing there with her camera raised. Geraldo was with her.

The guys cursed and ran.

"Too late for you, losers!" It was Lupe. She yelled after them, "I have pictures of you!"

They disappeared around the corner. Geraldo ran out of the store and raced after them. Just before they went around the corner, I saw him tackle Nathan.

A siren screamed, and a cop car came flying down the alley, headlights on high, speeding past the store, following them. It went around the corner and I heard it stop, then cops talking. There was more cursing and yelling, and some scuffling. Sounds of fighting. I could hear the cop car's radio, static and voices talking back and forth.

I got up, feeling hurt all over. Blood was pouring out of my nose, all over my chest.

14

Lupe was still standing in the doorway of the store.

I picked up my shirt and held it to my face to wipe off some of the blood.

"I got your note, Jacob," Lupe called to me. "I showed it to Officer Dassler this afternoon. And I got pictures of them breaking in."

"How did you get my note?"

"I saw you give it to Craig. I knew it was for me. I was curious. I had to know what you wrote. So I got my friend Rosa to ask Mr. Kloot a question after class, and while he was talking to her, I walked past the garbage can and grabbed it."

Just like I always said: the smartest kid in school. I wished I could hug her. I was so relieved. I walked over to her, limping because Nathan had kicked me in the kneecap.

She just looked at me, all serious. No hug.

"I'm sorry, Lupe," I said.

"I know," she said. "You're not really like that. I don't know what's wrong with you, but the Jacob I know isn't like that."

"Not anymore," I said. "I don't care if they beat me up every day. I don't care if they send me to jail. I don't want to be like them."

I looked down the alley, toward the cop noises coming from around the corner. Flashing red and blue lights bounced off the walls of the stores. The cops were talking on their radio. Otherwise, it was quiet. The cops had everything under control. They must have arrested Nathan and his buddies.

I didn't know what to do. Should I stay here? Go tell the cops I was with them? I was sick of hiding and lying.

"They're not going to arrest you," she said.

It was like she could read my mind.

"How do you know?"

"I showed Officer Dassler your note today when he came into the store. He knows you wanted to stop them. So I came here tonight to see what would happen. I waited upstairs in the store. I kept it dark so they wouldn't see me. Geraldo waited downstairs. I was the lookout. I stayed up here watching out the window. I knitted to keep myself awake in the dark, and I waited."

"Then, when I heard all the bottles get broken, I went downstairs and Geraldo and I waited behind the door. Also, I called Officer Dassler. He waited around the corner in his car until they broke in. He wanted to catch them doing it so he could really send them to jail."

"Also," she said, "I took pictures of them. But I didn't take any pictures of you at all. And Officer Dassler never saw you. So no one can prove you were ever here. You never went near the door of the store. Even if they lie and say you were doing it with them, the pictures show you weren't."

Smartest kid in school. She really was. No doubt about it.

I gave her a huge hug. This time, she let me.

"Lupe," I said, "I'm really sorry about all this. Will you go out with me again?"

"I don't know," she said. "I'll have to think about it. I'll have to watch you. If you really are going to be a good person again, then maybe. But it will take a while before I know for sure."

Life is like that, my dad would have said. On TV, stories end with everything being OK. In real life, you're not always sure. But I knew that from now on, I would do everything I could to make her believe in me.

15

The next day was Saturday, so there was no school, which was good. My face was a mess, and I was sore all over. My mother made me a milkshake for breakfast, because I couldn't eat regular food. My mouth hurt too much from being punched.

I told her everything. About how I was scared, and mad. About all the trouble I got into with Nathan and his gang.

"You'll have to pay for those windows you broke," she said. "And the camera at the first store. And wash off that writing behind the car wash."

"I know," I said. "I will."

As soon as we finished breakfast, my mom and I went to the hospital. People there stared at me because of my beat-up face, but not too much. I guess they expected to see beat-up, hurt-looking people in the hospital.

We watched my dad sleep. Watched machines beep and light up their numbers.

My dad was breathing peacefully. Like he wasn't in pain, and nothing was bothering him.

The doctor came in. Uh-oh. What bad news would she bring this time?

The doctor touched my dad's arm. "Mr. Gardner?"

My dad woke up. "Hey, Jacob! Nice to see you!" was the first thing he said. "What happened to your face?"

"I got in a fight," I said.

The doctor coughed, like she didn't want to talk about that. She said, "I have some good news for all of you. Mr. Gardner, you can go home later today. We're arranging a nurse to come to your house and give you your treatment."

She and my mom and dad talked some more. A lot of medical stuff, which I didn't understand. Was he still going to die? The doctor said she didn't know. Things still didn't look good. But my dad would definitely live longer than without the treatment.

And he would be better enough to come home. We were all excited about that.

After the doctor left, my dad asked me about my face again. "What happened?" he asked.

I told him everything. About the gang of bullies, and my life of crime. About Lupe, and how smart she was. The smartest kid in school. She had saved me.

"Everyone does stupid things sometimes," my dad said. "What matters is that now you know they're stupid, and you're not going to do them anymore. And your mom is right. You'll have to pay for all the damage you did."

I nodded. I felt so wrung out, like an old washcloth. Now that they both knew, I could finally relax.

After a while, my mom motioned to me to move my chair over next to her, next to my dad's bed, and lean my head on her shoulder. I did, and she hugged me for the longest time. Not saying anything. But she didn't need to.

My dad reached out from the hospital bed and put his hand on my arm.

I was so glad he was going to come home. To fill in the empty place in our house.

We were all quiet. That was one thing I really liked about my parents. You could be quiet with them, and it was OK.

I took a deep breath, and finally fell asleep, right there in the hospital chair.

We were together again.

I didn't know how long it would last, but I promised myself I would save this memory forever.

My mom, my dad, and me. And maybe, just maybe, Lupe.

About The Author

Kelly Winters is a part-time writer and a full-time mom. She homeschools her son, who struggles with reading comprehension, so contributing a story to the first Story Share contest was important to her! She is honored to be a part of any endeavor that helps kids become more interested and able readers.

About The Publisher

Story Shares is a nonprofit focused on supporting the millions of teens and adults who struggle with reading by creating a new shelf in the library specifically for them. The ever-growing collection features content that is compelling and culturally relevant for teens and adults, yet still readable at a range of lower reading levels.

Story Shares generates content by engaging deeply with writers, bringing together a community to create this new kind of book. With more intriguing and approachable stories to choose from, the teens and adults who have fallen behind are improving their skills and beginning to discover the joy of reading. For more information, visit storyshares.org.

Easy to Read. Hard to Put Down.

www.ingramcontent.com/pod-product-compliance
Lightning Source LLC
Chambersburg PA
CBHW071221170626
46809CB00005BA/1894